My Sister, Then and Now

My Sister,
Then and Now

by Virginia L. Kroll

illustrations by
Mary Worcester

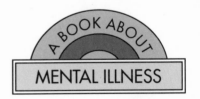

A BOOK ABOUT
MENTAL ILLNESS

CAROLRHODA BOOKS
MINNEAPOLIS. MINNESOTA USA

The publisher wishes to thank Dr. Elizabeth Reeve
of the Division of Child and Adolescent Psychiatry
at the University of Minnesota for her assistance
in the preparation of this book.

This book is available in two editions:
Library edition by Carolrhoda Books, Inc.
Soft cover by First Avenue Editions
241 First Avenue North
Minneapolis, Minnesota 55401

Library of Congress Cataloging-in-Publication Data

Kroll, Virginia L.
    My sister, then and now / by Virginia L. Kroll ; illustrations by
Mary Worcester.
        p.   cm.
    Summary: Ten-year-old Rachael describes how her twenty-year-
old sister's schizophrenia has affected the family and expresses
her own feelings of sadness and anger.
    ISBN 0-87614-718-X (lib. bdg.)
    ISBN 0-87614-584-5 (pbk.)
    [1. Schizophrenia—Fiction. 2. Mentally ill—Fiction.]
I. Worcester, Mary, ill. II. Title.
PZ7.K9227My   1992   91-31297
[Fic]—dc20   CIP
                                                                AC
Manufactured in the United States of America

1 2 3 4 5 6 7 8 9 10 01 00 99 98 97 96 95 94 93 92

Many thanks to
Steven P. Herman, M.D.
Laurence R. Plumb, M.D.
and
Bonnie J. Collins, Ed.M., C.S.W.
for their friendship and professional help.
To them I dedicate this book.

My sister and I used to gather pussy willows in the springtime. In the summer, my sister would drive me to the beach, and we would feed the seagulls and lick ice-cream cones together. In the fall, we would pile up leaves and jump into them. In the winter, we would build snow-block forts until our hands were numb and then come inside to drink hot cocoa with peppermint drops melted in it.

I was born when Karen was ten. And even though my friends fight with their brothers and sisters all the time, Karen and I hardly ever did. She always seemed too old to fight with, so we were friends instead. She was my big sister then, and I looked up to her.

But now *I'm* ten, and it seems like I'm the older one. I didn't expect it to be this way, and I don't like the upside-down feeling it gives me. You see, my sister is mentally ill.

For a long time, we knew something was wrong with Karen, but we didn't know what. She and I used to share a bedroom, and when I was nine, she started waking me up at night. I'd find her standing in the dark, staring at me and crying. She'd cry and say things like "I wonder if I did OK on my exam," and "What if my hair starts falling out?" and "The moon doesn't like me anymore." She was scared of lots of things, and she started scaring me, too. Finally my parents moved me to a different room.

First Daddy said, "It must be stress," because Karen had just started college. But then she started thinking that people were putting poison in her food. She lost a lot of weight because she didn't want to eat. Our family doctor said Karen had had a nervous breakdown. After a few months, she dropped out of school.

More and more, it seemed like Karen was living in a make-believe world. One time she screamed that there was a huge tarantula on the wall, but really it was only a tiny house spider. Another time, when we were home alone, she went outside in a snowstorm without a coat. She said a voice told her to do it, but it wasn't me.

My parents took Karen to special doctors for lots of tests. Finally they gave her sickness a name. They called it *schizophrenia* (SKIT-soh-FREE-nee-ah). It's a big word, but I've heard it said so many times that it doesn't seem big to me anymore. I even know how to spell it.

Schizophrenia is a strange disease. Sometimes it makes people hear voices inside their heads. Sometimes they can't tell what's real and what isn't. Sometimes it makes nice people crabby and calm people nervous. Sometimes it makes people imagine that other people are trying to hurt them.

After we found out what was wrong with Karen, my parents cried a lot. I tried to cheer them up, but even when I made pudding or washed the kitchen floor or got three A's on my report card, they didn't notice like they used to. All they thought about was Karen. "Why did it happen?" they asked over and over again.

Karen started taking medicine to calm her down and help her think straight. For a while, it felt like our family was back to normal. But then my sister thought she was better and stopped taking her medicine. She still stops taking it sometimes, and without it she always gets bad again. I just wish there was a magic pill she could take once and for all to make her better.

I didn't tell my friends about Karen. I hoped they wouldn't notice. But once in the grocery store when my friend Roger and his dad were there, my sister made faces at the check-out clerk. After that my friend Jacqueline said, "My mother thinks we should play at my house instead of yours." I said OK, but inside I felt sad, and later I cried.

Another day my best friend, Maria, was over, and Karen was in one of her crabby moods. Karen told Maria, "You have a big baboon nose" and laughed in her face. Maria had always hated her nose, and Karen's words made Maria cry.

After that I didn't dare invite anyone over. I didn't want them to see how weird my sister was acting. That made me mad, because all the other kids could have people over— everyone except me.

"It's not fair! She's ruining everything!" I screamed at my parents.

"No," Mama said. "Her illness is ruining everything."

Daddy said, "If Karen had cancer, you'd feel bad for her. You'd want to be kind and helpful."

"But she doesn't have cancer, and I wish she did have it instead of what she does have. Then she wouldn't be mean and scary. She'd just be sick," I said.

Mama said, "Your sister can't help it—"

"That person is not my sister!" I yelled. I ran out and slammed the door.

One day Mama said, "Rachael, I'd like you to see a counselor. I've made an appointment for Wednesday after school."

"That's not fair," I argued. "I'm not the sick one!"

Mama told me that Karen's disease affects our whole family and that talking about it might help me. She said it helps her to talk about it, because sometimes she gets mad at Karen, too. I was glad to know Mama felt the same way, and I told her I'd go see the counselor.

Dr. Collins had short, red hair and a happy face. She and I looked at some books and played with Legos at first. Then, instead of asking me about school and the weather like I expected her to, she got right to the point. "So, Rachael, tell me why you're here," she said.

I answered politely, "My sister is mentally ill, and my mom thinks I should talk to you about it."

"What do you think?" Dr. Collins asked.

"I don't know," I said, shrugging.

Dr. Collins didn't say anything. She didn't have to. She just looked at me, and something in her face made me say everything I had said to my parents and more. Suddenly I was crying and slamming the books on the floor and shouting, "I hate her!" over and over.

When I finally calmed down, I was surprised that Dr. Collins was still looking at me in a nice way. "I guess you think I'm really mean," I said.

"Not at all," answered Dr. Collins.

"Well, I don't *really* hate her," I explained. I just wish Karen would go back to the way she used to be."

"I know what you mean," Dr. Collins said. "I have a brother who is mentally ill. It was hard to accept that he is different from how he used to be. But people with mental illnesses still lead normal lives. My brother has a family and goes to work just like I do."

We built a Lego house while we talked about her brother. Finally I asked the question I had wanted to ask for a long time. "Can I catch it from my sister, like you catch a cold or the flu or strep throat?"

"No, not at all," Dr. Collins replied. "Sometimes more than one person in the same family is mentally ill, and sometimes there's only one. There's a lot we *don't* know about mental illness, but we *do* know that you can't catch it from someone else, like you might catch a cold."

I felt better when I left Dr. Collins's office. I was glad I'd get to see her again the next week.

That night I came down with the flu. My face was hot, but my body felt cold. For three days, my throat hurt so badly I couldn't swallow. It even hurt to eat ice cream.

All I could do was lie in bed and think. I thought that when I grow up, I'd like to be a counselor. Then I could help sisters and brothers of mentally ill people just like Dr. Collins is helping me.

I thought even longer about my being sick and how I didn't really have a choice. I didn't *want* a fever and chills and a sore throat. The flu was just something that happened to me.

I understand now that mental illness is the same way. My sister didn't choose to feel and act the way she does. It just happened to her. But it happened in her brain instead of in her body, and she didn't catch it from anyone. She won't get over it as easily as I got over the flu, either.

Now in the springtime, I gather pussy willows by myself and put them in a vase for my sister. In the summer, we stay home and scatter bread for the pigeons and drink lemonade. In the fall, I pile up leaves, but since Karen won't jump into them, I do it myself and remember how much fun we used to have. In the winter, I see her staring into space with blank eyes while I build snow-block forts. When I come inside, I make hot cocoa for both of us, but she thinks the peppermint drops could be medicine, so I leave them out.

So many things have changed. I still have a sister. But now my sister is mentally ill. I'll try to keep loving her, even on the days when she acts like she hates me. My family and I will keep caring for her just like we do when anyone else is sick. And someday, if doctors learn as much about schizophrenia as they know about the flu and strep throat, maybe my sister will get better and be just like she was—then.

ABOUT THE AUTHOR

Virginia L. Kroll has written hundreds of articles for children's magazines and recently has extended her writing abilities to children's books. When she is not writing, she keeps busy caring for her six children—who range in age from 3 to 22—and her 1-year-old granddaughter. Her constant exposure to children of all ages as a mother and a former elementary school teacher provides her with a reservoir brimming with new ideas. Ms. Kroll lives in Hamburg, New York.

ABOUT THE ILLUSTRATOR

Mary Worcester received a bachelor of fine arts degree from Columbus College of Art and Design in 1981. She now lives in Minneapolis, Minnesota, where she is a free-lance artist. In addition to her many advertising projects, she has also created covers for several adult books. This is her first book for children.